Good Times with the Molesons

Good Times with the Molesons

Stories by **Burny Bos**

Illustrated by **Hans de Beer**

Translated by J. Alison James

North-South Books

New York / London

First published in Switzerland under the title *Familie Maulwurf Herzlichen Glückwunsch!*

First published in the United States, Great Britain, Canada,
Australia, and New Zealand in 2001 by North-South Books,
an imprint of Nord-Süd Verlag AG, Gossau Zürich, Switzerland.

Distributed in the United States by North-South Books Inc., New York.

Library of Congress Cataloging-in-Publication Data is available.
A CIP catalogue record for this book is available from The British Library.
ISBN 0-7358-1519-4 (trade binding)
1 3 5 7 9 TB 10 8 6 4 2
ISBN 0-7358-1520-8 (library binding)
1 3 5 7 9 LB 10 8 6 4 2
Printed in Belgium

For more information about our books, and the authors and artists
who create them, visit our web site: www.northsouth.com

Contents

Meet the Molesons	7
At the Pool	8
At the Dentist	15
The Birthday Party	20
A Trip in the Car	26
By the Fireside	31
Grandma in the Snow	37
Just a Normal Family	44

Meet the Molesons

This is my family, the Molesons. We're pretty ordinary: mother, father, sister, brother—oh, and Grandma—can't forget her. You might remember the time when this picture was taken—Father was trying to be a gymnast and got stuck in a back bend! I'm sure your father would do the same. Mother took him to the doctor on a wheelbarrow. Just like any mother, of course.

But in case you don't know us, let me tell you a little more. My mother carries the briefcase in this family. Father gets things done around the house. My name is Dug. Dusty is my twin sister. We go to school, like most kids our age. Grandma is amazing. She can race any bicycle with her electric wheelchair—and win.

Like I say, we're just your normal, run-of-the-mill family.

At the Pool

One day Mother and Father decided to take us swimming.

Mother pulled an old swimsuit out of a drawer. "Just look at this!" She started laughing. "I can't believe this used to fit me!"

Father nodded seriously at Mother and said, "Yes indeed! You have put on some weight there."

Mother stopped laughing. "And you haven't?" she shot back.

Dusty and I looked at each other from the doorway. They sounded like us!

Father turned a little pink. He patted his belly and said, "It's all muscle. I'm as fit as ever."

Dusty and I ran to our room giggling.

A short time later, we were all at the pool.

"Come on in, children. You won't get in shape just standing there!" Father climbed up the steps to the high diving board. "Look, this is what you do." He jumped up and down on the end of the board. He jumped and jumped and jumped.

The lifeguard blew his whistle. "Take your dive!"

Father tried to do a swan dive, but he landed smack on his belly. A loud *crack!* echoed all around us. Then a cry: "AAAOOOWWW!!"

Father crawled out of the pool. His belly hurt. He gasped for breath.

The lifeguard came over. “From now on, the high dive is off limits for you,” he said sternly. “I can’t believe an adult would play around like that!”

Mother and Dusty came over.

Mother said, “What did the lifeguard say?”

“Was he really mad?” Dusty asked.

"Oh," Father said. "I just can't dive from the high board again. Who cares!" And without a glance, he jumped right in. Splash! A wave of water went over Mother's head.

Mother spluttered and coughed. "Children," she said, "give me a hand. Your father needs to learn a lesson."

So Dusty and I jumped in and gave Father a good dunking.

At the Dentist

It was our day to go to the dentist. We all went together. Father went first.

The dentist looked at every one of his teeth. “Looks good,” the dentist said.

“Wonderful,” Father said, bouncing from the chair. “See?” he said to me. “It wasn’t so bad.”

Dusty was next. She didn’t need any fillings either. “What luck!” She sighed.

"Next?" said the dentist.

I was supposed to be next. But I didn't want to go. I felt ill.

"I'll go next then," Mother offered. Soon she was sitting back in the chair. All her teeth were fine as well.

Now there was nobody left but me. Reluctantly I lay back in the chair.

"It's never as bad as it seems," Father said.

"Whatever you say, Father," I said.

I lay nice and still until the dentist said, "Oh, here's a little one!"

Why me? Why always me? I always get the bad luck! I jumped up from the chair and tried to run for it.

The dentist grabbed me and tried to hold me back.

"NO! NO! NO!" I screamed.

"It won't hurt a bit," promised the dentist.

"No!" I cried. "I don't want to!"

Then Father had an idea. He lay back in the chair himself. "Now, come here, son," he said.

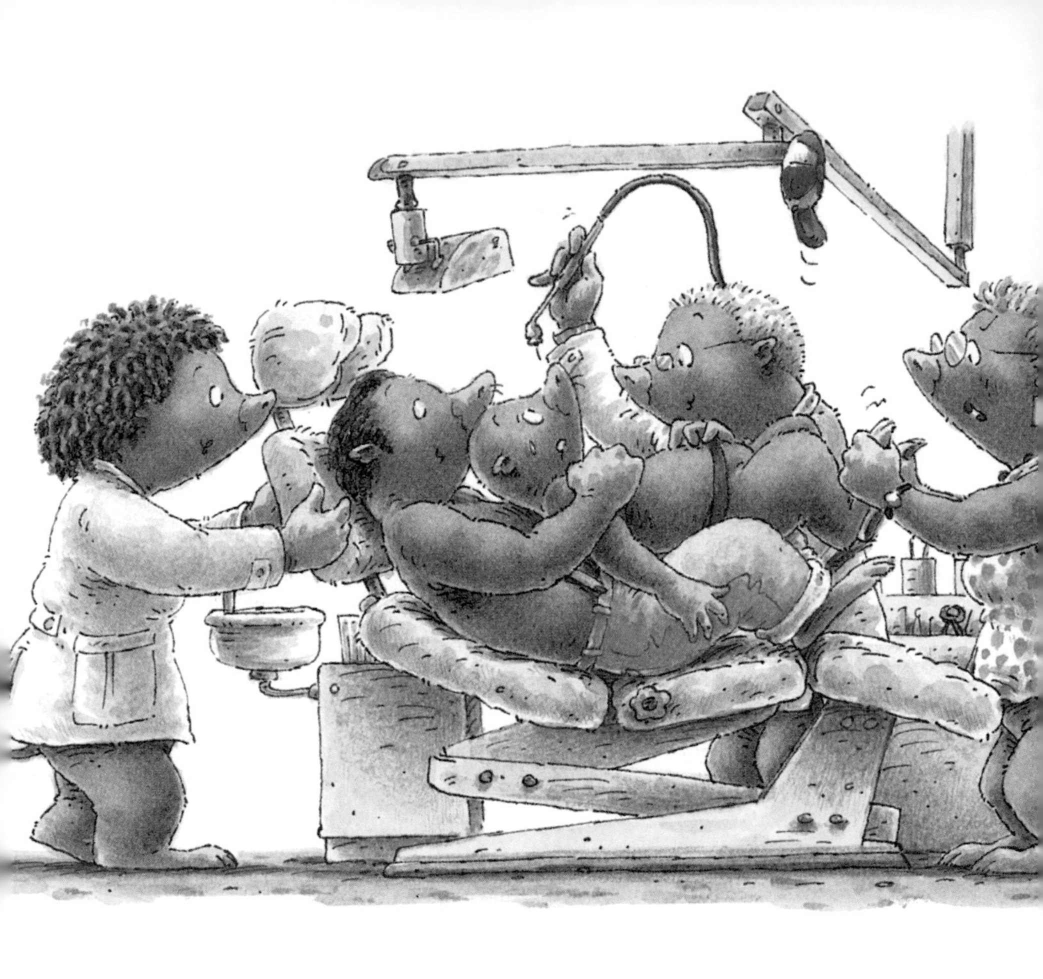

I climbed up on top of Father. Father hugged me close. Mother rubbed my feet. Dusty made funny faces at me. The dentist filled the cavity.

Then it was all over. I was okay. I rubbed the tears from my face. "It really didn't hurt," I told Dusty.

"We can do it the same way next time," said Father.

The Birthday Party

It was Father's birthday. But nobody had wished him a happy birthday. We didn't forget—we were all still asleep. It was six in the morning!

Father wanted to paint the fence before the guests came. He would have to work hard to get it done in one day.

All day Father painted and painted.

Inside, we got ready for the party. We put up decorations. We made the cake. We made lots of delicious food for the guests. All of Father's friends would be here. We were so excited.

Finally Father came in from painting the fence. Dusty and I sang "Happy Birthday" to him. He covered up a yawn with his hand.

Maybe we need to work on our singing.

At last the guests arrived. Everyone was there—even Grandma. Only the birthday boy didn't join in the fun.

Father was stretched out in his comfortable chair, snoring away.

The guests started to laugh. He looked so happy, nobody wanted to bother him. They went ahead and enjoyed the party. Father was left in peace.

It was bedtime when Father woke up. "Humpf!" he said, gulping back a snore. "When do the guests come?"

Mother showed him the table. All the presents were there. All the food had been eaten. There was a small plate of birthday cake that she'd saved for Father.

"Your guests have all come and gone," she said.

"How embarrassing," groaned father. "I'm so ashamed."

"At least the fence is done," Grandma said.

"And at last Father has had enough sleep!" I said. He always complained about being too tired.

Then Father laughed, and we all sang Happy Birthday and helped him open his presents.

A Trip in the Car

"We're going for a weekend in the city!" Mother said, beaming with pleasure.

"Oh boy!" I cried. "Can we fly?"

"Yes," cried Dusty. "We've never flown before."

Father shook his head. "It's much too expensive to fly," he said. "We'll take the car.

Dusty and I sat in the backseat, feeling grumpy. "We always have to take the car," Dusty complained.

I called up to the front, "How much longer will it take?"

Dusty said, "We'd already be there if we had taken the plane."

Mother looked angrily over her shoulder. "Enough from both of you. We've been on the road for an hour now. In five more hours we'll be in the city."

The car made a knocking noise.

"What's that?" Mother asked. "Is that normal?"

"Of course it is," said Father. "It's only . . . uh . . ."

Suddenly the noise got louder. It sounded as if someone had thrown a crate of nails into the engine.

Dusty said, "Sounds bad."

"It's just the road, children," Father said.

But then the car went *crack!* and stopped.

"It's going to take a lot of work," said the mechanic after he checked the engine.

Father looked at the broken engine. He was fed up. "That will cost a fortune," he growled.

Soon we were on our way again. We got to ride piggyback! It was fantastic!

I asked "Is it still a long way to the city?"

"Very long," Mother said. "It's the other direction. We have to go home since the car is broken."

Mother was angry, but Dusty and I weren't. Riding up high like this was almost as good as going in an airplane.

"Hey, Father!" Dusty said. "We're almost flying, but we didn't need to buy airplane tickets!"

But Father didn't answer. He just glared at us.

By the Fireside

"Isn't our new fireplace lovely!" Mother said.

Father had just finished building it.

Mother had an idea. "Tonight we'll have family time around the fireplace. We can tell stories and sing songs."

So that evening Father made a great big fire in the fireplace. Dusty and I sat in front of it all warm from our baths. Everyone looked at the fire.

Mother sniffed. "Doesn't it smell a bit like smoke in here?" she asked.

"Where there's smoke, there's fire," Father said. "And we've certainly got a fire!" He fanned the flames to make it burn better.

Dusty held her nose. So did I. It really did smell bad.

My eyes started to burn. Mother coughed. "If you ask me," she said, "the fire doesn't seem to be burning properly."

We almost couldn't see each other through the smoke.

Father looked up the chimney.

Tears streamed down my face. Our fire was getting smaller and smaller.

"Something is not right," Father said.

Mother ran to the kitchen. She came back with a watering can. She poured water on the fire.

Father opened the door to the garden. A cold wind blew the smoke outside.

"This is supposed to be warm?" I asked.

"I'm freezing!" Dusty whimpered.

"Oh, it's nothing," Mother said. "If we put on our jackets, we won't notice the cold."

So we sat there in front of the fireplace, wearing our heavy coats and hats.

Father passed the juice around and Mother shared the snacks. We were all trying as hard as we could to have a good time.

"I'm really sleepy," I lied. I wanted to be tucked into my warm bed. It was too cold.

Even Mother was shivering. So she took Dusty and me upstairs.

When Father was on his own, he noticed a little handle on the side of the fireplace.

He pulled it down. The flue opened up. The air drew up the chimney. Father lit a fire. All the smoke went up the chimney.

"Everyone, come quickly!" he shouted.

We thought the house was on fire. We all jumped out of bed and ran downstairs.

Father was sitting in front of a crackling fire. It was so warm and snug that we sat there and watched the flames until Dusty and I fell asleep.

Grandma in the Snow

"Get a move on!" cried Grandma. "Hurry up!"

Dusty and I were pushing her through the snow on our walk.

She took a deep breath. "Umm! Heavenly fresh air! The snow is so beautiful!"

We pushed as hard as we could.

But the snow was too deep.

"Grandma," I said, "I can't push anymore."

"I am so tired," Dusty said.

"Time for the rocket boosters," Grandma said cheerfully. She didn't like to use up her battery when we could push.

She turned on her wheelchair motor. The wheels spun around. They made deep tracks in the snow, but the chair didn't move.

"Now we have a problem," Grandma said. She looked around. There were no other people anywhere. Only snow.

Dusty took my hand. We were scared. It was already getting dark.

"We passed a house back there," Grandma said. "You two run and ask for help."

We ran. We ran as fast as we could. We followed our tracks through the snow.

I kept looking back. Grandma looked so tiny. She sat there all alone in her chair.

It started to snow.

"Grandma must be freezing," Dusty said.

I just grunted. We ran faster.

At last we saw lights. It was the house. We could smell their fire burning. Dusty pounded on the door. "Help!" she cried. "Please help us!"

"Grandma! Grandma!" I called, but she couldn't hear me. The tractor engine was too noisy.

Dusty and I had found a lady at the house. She was a farmer, and she had a tractor. She was glad to help.

The farmer tied a rope onto Grandma's wheelchair and fastened it to the tractor. Then she pulled Grandma smoothly through the snow, right back to the road.

"We'll be fine now," Grandma said. "Thank you so very much for your help!"

"All right, you two, hop up!" Grandma said. "I need a little warmth."

We snuggled up on Grandma's lap and zipped along the road. Grandma sang a song. She was happy. It wasn't every day she got a tow from a tractor!

Just a Normal Family

Just because our stories are in a book, you might think that the Moleson family is special. But we're not. Things must be much more exciting at your house. You really ought to write about your family. I mean, if I can, so can you.

About the Author

Burny Bos was born in Haarlem, in the Netherlands. He began his career as a teacher, and in 1973 he started developing children's shows for Dutch radio. Within a few years he was working for Dutch television as well. He has won many prizes for his children's broadcasts, films, and recordings. He has also written over two dozen children's books, including *Alexander the Great* and the earlier adventures of the Molesons: *Meet the Molesons*, *More from the Molesons*, *Leave It to the Molesons!*, and *Fun with the Molesons*.

About the Artist

Hans de Beer was born in Muiden, a small town near Amsterdam, in the Netherlands. He began to draw when he went to school, mostly when the lessons got too boring. He studied illustration at the Rietveld Academy of Art in Amsterdam.

Hans de Beer is the author and illustrator of the popular series of picture books featuring Lars, the Little Polar Bear, which have been published in eighteen languages around the world. He has illustrated many other books, including *Alexander the Great* and the first four books about the Molesons.

DON'T MISS
THE OTHER BOOKS
IN THIS SERIES:

Meet the Molesons

•

More from the Molesons

•

Leave It to the Molesons!

•

Fun with the Molesons